# THE QUEEN'S HAT

Steve Antony

For Mum, Dad and Joseph.
Without you, this book wouldn't exist.

First published in 2014 by Hodder Children's Books

Copyright © Steve Antony 2014

Hodder Children's Books, 338 Euston Road, London, NW1 3BH
Hodder Children's Books Australia, Level 17/207 Kent Street,
Sydney, NSW 2000

The right of Steve Antony to be identified as the author and illustrator
of this Work has been asserted by him in accordance with the Copyright,
Designs and Patents Act 1988.

A catalogue record of this book is available from the British Library.

ISBN 978 1 444 91914 1

Printed in China

Hodder Children's Books is a division
of Hachette Children's Books,
an Hachette UK Company

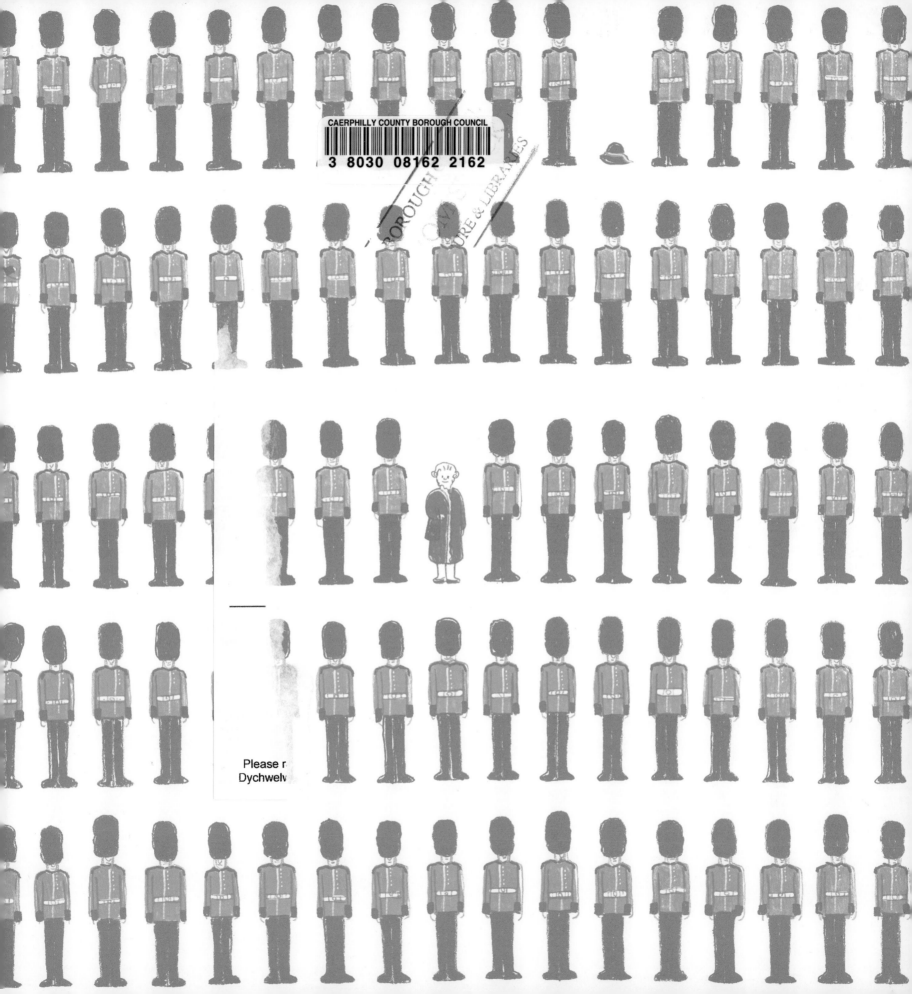

Please r
Dychwel

# THE QUEEN'S HAT

Steve Antony

Hodder
Children's
Books

A division of Hachette Children's Books

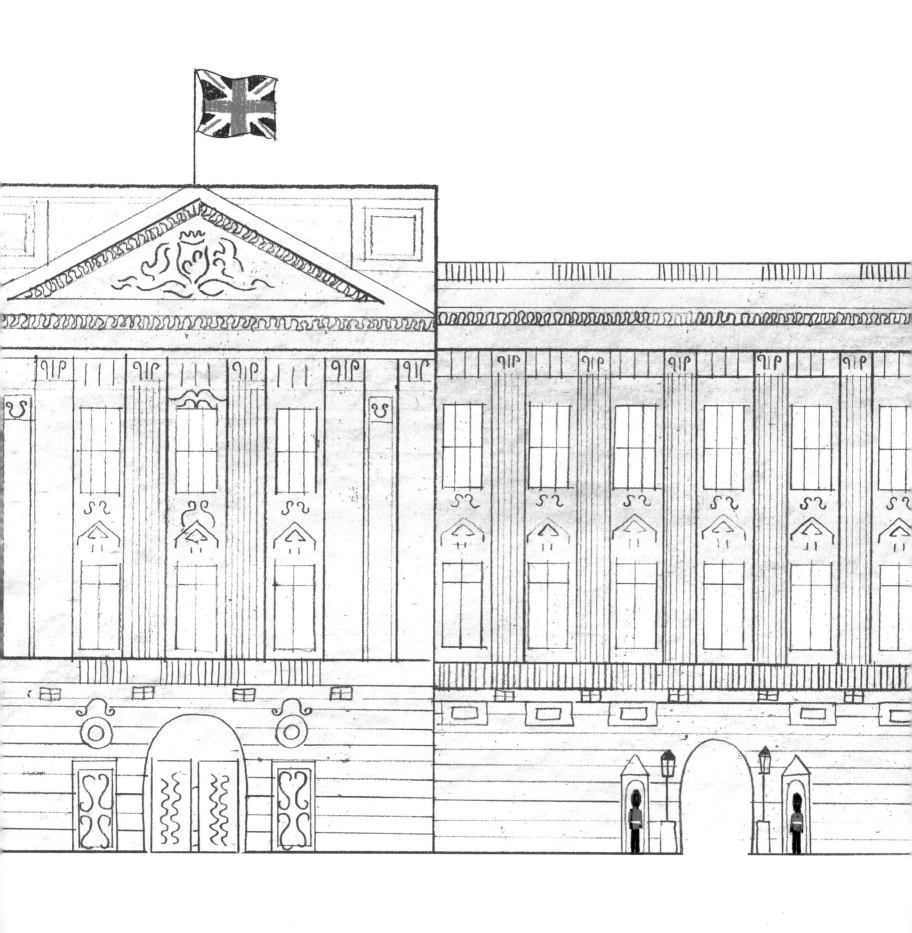

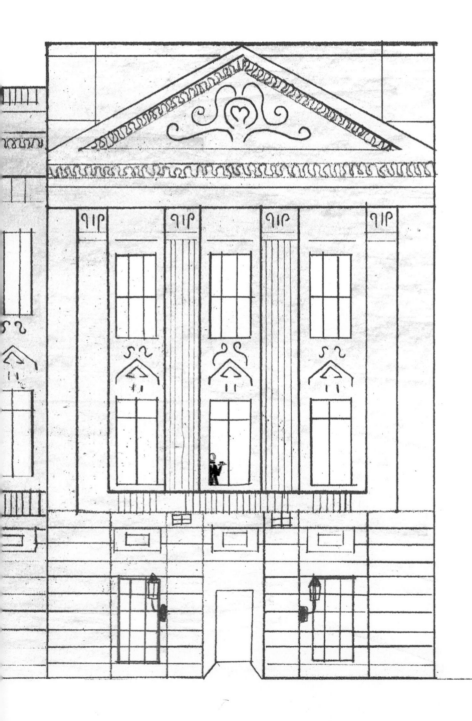

The Queen was on her way to visit someone very special when the wind went...

# swish!

The wind took the Queen's favourite hat right off her head.

It soared high above the Queen.
It wooshed high above the Queen's men.

The wind was so strong that it
swept the Queen's hat all the way to...

Trafalgar Square...

and all through...

London Zoo...

and all along...

the London Underground...

and all around...

the London Eye...

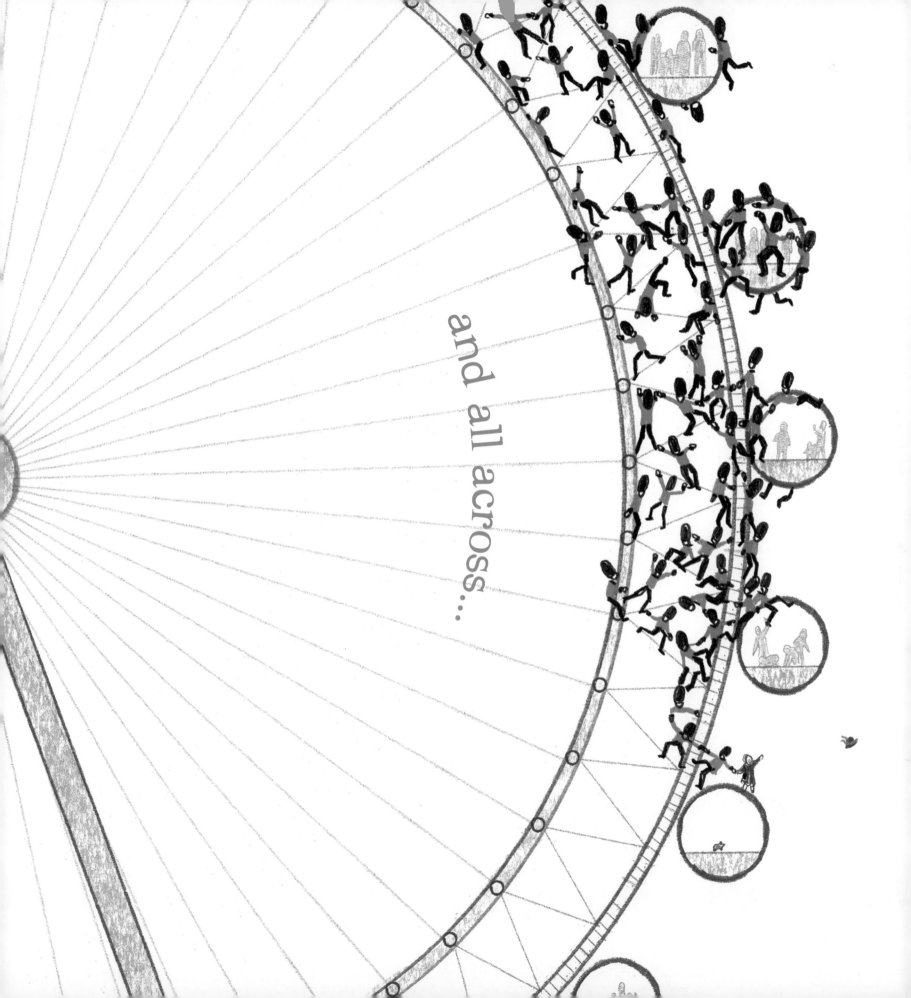

and all across...

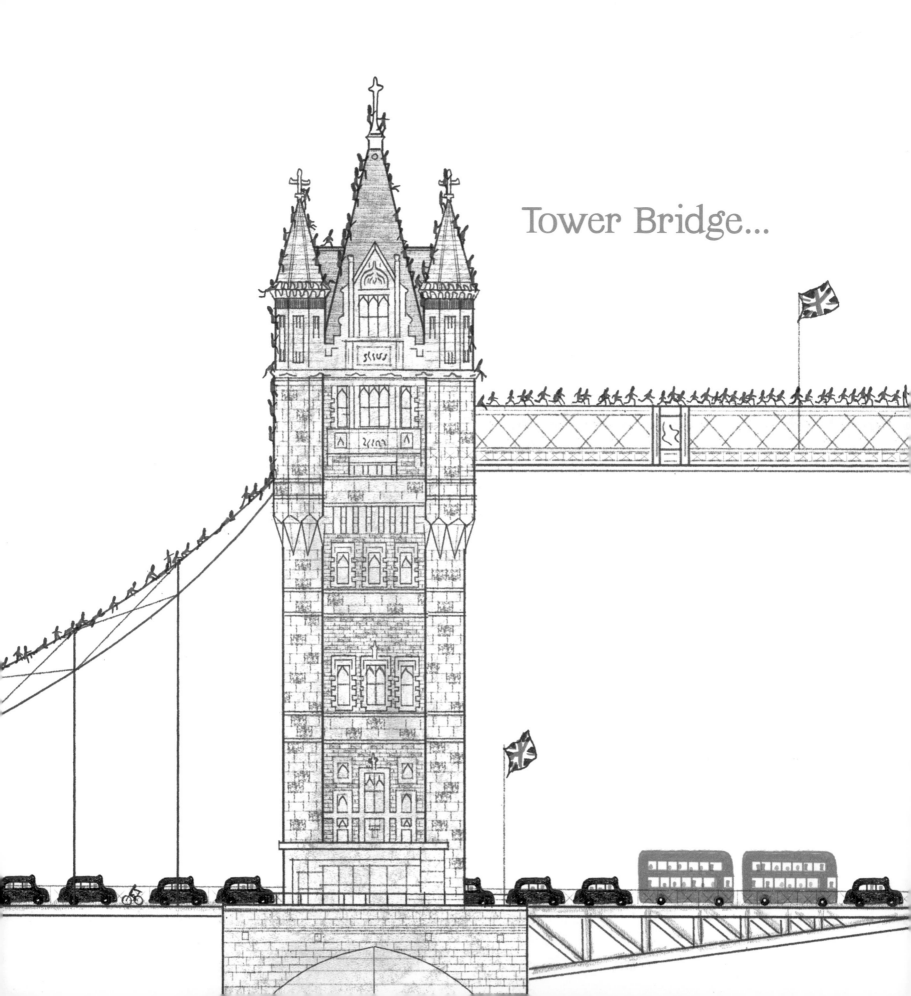

Tower Bridge...

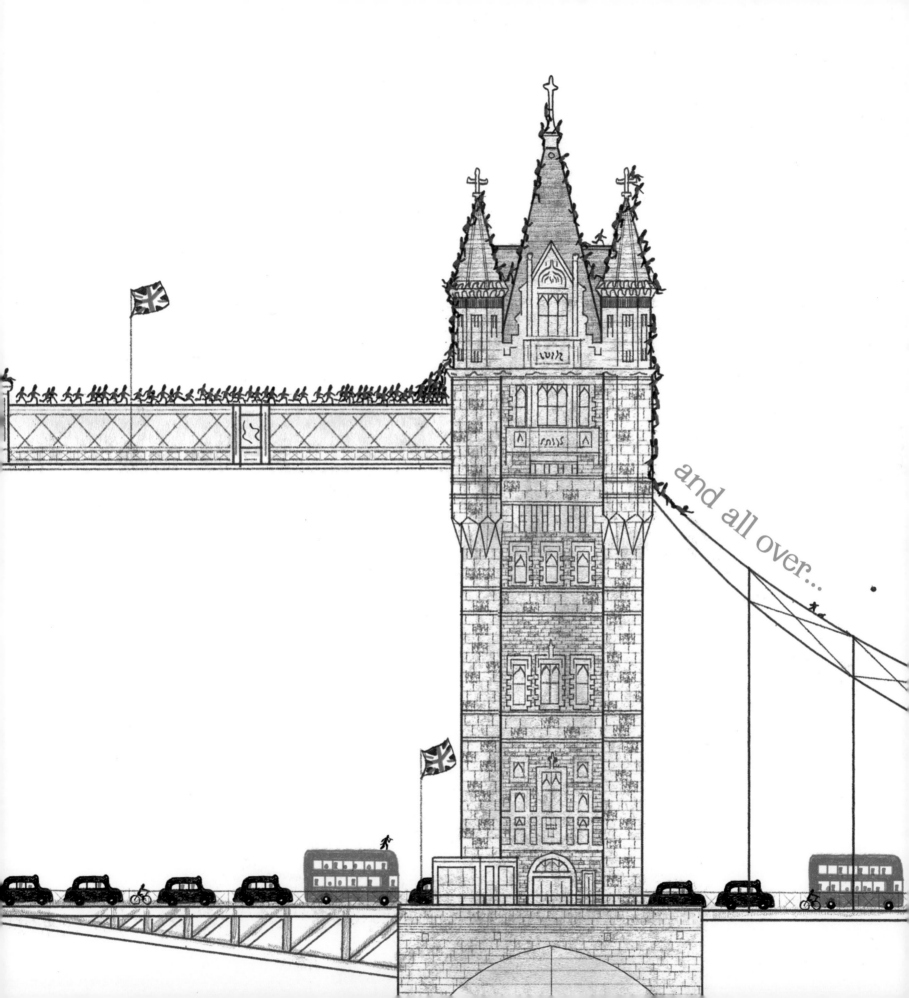

and all over...

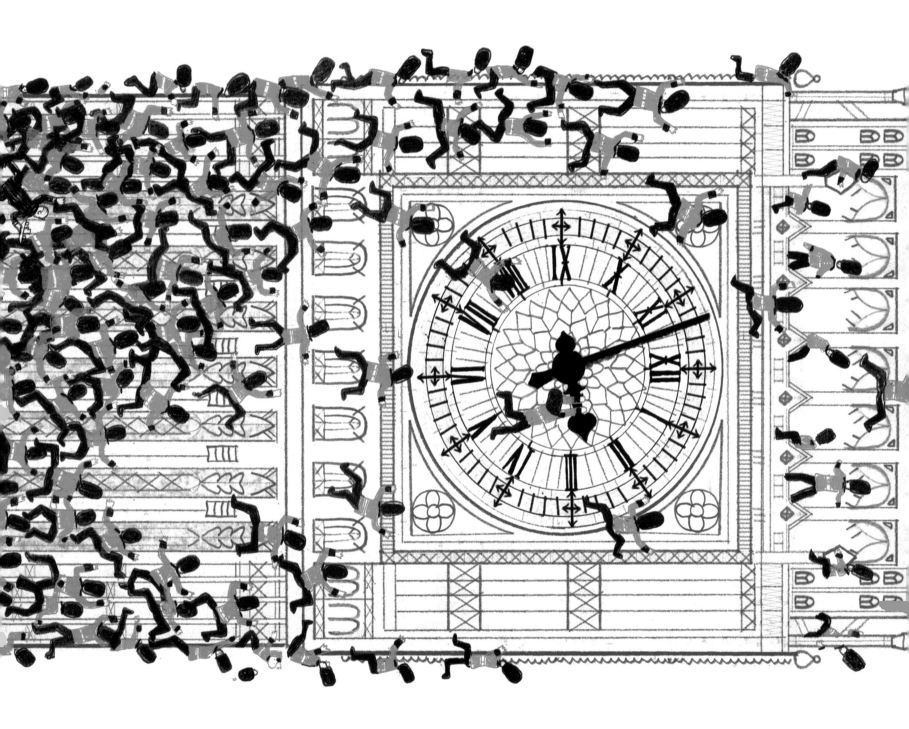

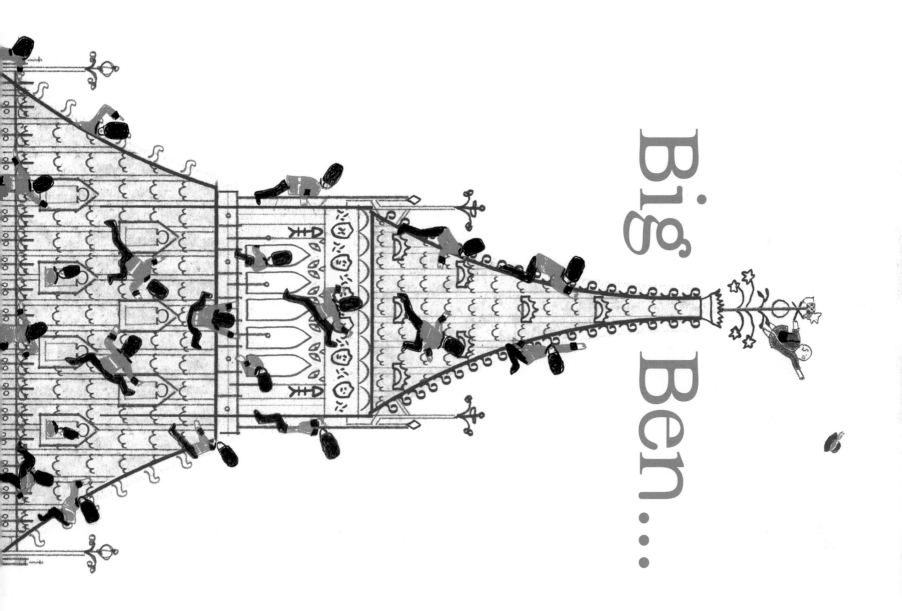

Big Ben....

where it sailed up further into the sky...

swooosh!

Until, at last, the Queen and all the Queen's men...

floated gently down...

to Kensington Palace...

along with the Queen's...

...hat!

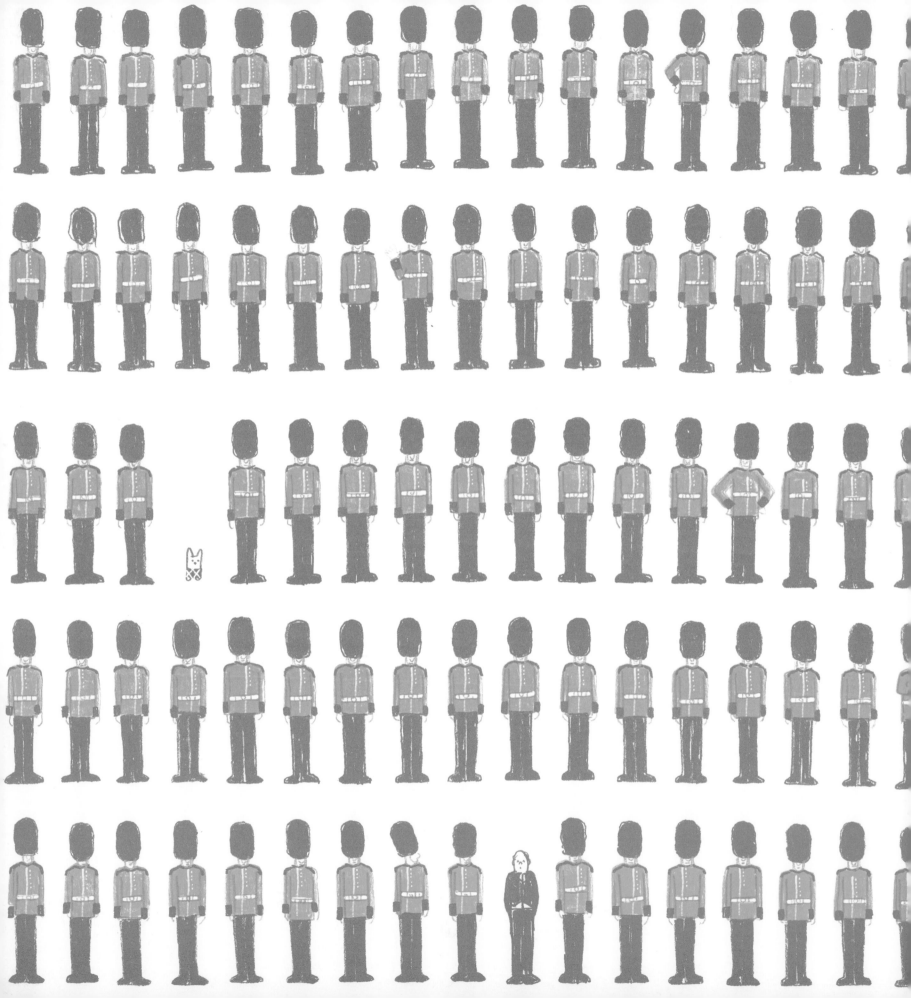